-HAUNTED HISTORY-

THE WHITE HOUSE IS HAUNTED!

MARIE MORRISON

PowerKiDS press.

NEW YORK

Published in 2021 by The Rosen Publishing Group, Inc.
29 East 21st Street, New York, NY 10010

Portions of this work were originally authored by Michael Rajczak and published as *Haunted! The White House.* All new material this edition authored by Marie Morrison.

Editor: Jill Keppeler
Book Design: Rachel Rising

Photo Credits: Cover, trekandshoot/Shutterstock.com; Cover, pp. 1–32 (background) Slava Gerj/Shutterstock.com; p. 5 AR Pictures/Shutterstock.com; p. 6 bauhaus1000/DigitalVision Vectors/Getty Images; p. 7 Chip Somodevilla/Staff/Getty Images; p. 9 Morphart Creation/Shutterstock.com; p. 11 Library of Congress Prints and Photographs Division: p. 13 Everett Historical/Shutterstock.com; p. 15 Harvey Meston/Staff/Getty Images; p. 17 Engel Ching/Shutterstock.com; p. 18 Pete Souza/The LIFE Picture Collection/Getty Images; p. 19 Win McNamee/Staff/Getty Images; p. 20 SAUL LOEB/AFP/Getty Images; p. 21 Hulton Archive/Stringer/Getty Images; p. 22 Zuzha/Shutterstock.com; p. 23 emkaplin/Shutterstock.com; p. 24 DEA/BIBLIOTECA AMBROSIANA/Contributor/Getty Images; p. 25 Erik Cox Photography/Shutterstock.com; p. 27 Dmitri Kessel/The LIFE Images Collection/Getty Image; p. 29 Orhan Cam/Shutterstock.com; p. 30 Lux Blue/Shutterstock.com.

Cataloging-in-Publication Data

Names: Morrison, Marie.
Title: The White House is haunted! / Marie Morrison.
Description: New York : PowerKids Press, 2021. | Series: Haunted history | Includes glossary and index.
Identifiers: ISBN 9781725320086 (pbk.) | ISBN 9781725320109 (library bound) | ISBN 9781725320093 (6 pack)
Subjects: LCSH: White House (Washington, D.C.)--Juvenile literature. | Haunted houses (Washington (D.C.)--Juvenile literature. | Ghosts--Washington (D.C.)--Juvenile literature. | Haunted places--Juvenile literature. | Washington (D.C.)--Buildings, structures, etc.--Juvenile literature.
Classification: LCC BF1475.M67 2021 | DDC 133.1--dc23

Manufactured in the United States of America

Some of the images in this book illustrate individuals who are models. The depictions do not imply actual situations or events.

CPSIA Compliance Information: Batch #CSPK20. For further information contact Rosen Publishing, New York, New York at 1-800-237-9932.

CONTENTS

WHITE HOUSE HISTORY

Since 1800, the large white building at 1600 Pennsylvania Avenue in Washington, D.C., has been the home and office of the president of the United States. Every president but George Washington has lived there. Both great and terrible things have taken place within its walls, and very important decisions have been made there.

With all that history, it's no surprise that there are many ghost stories connected to this, the oldest federal building in Washington, D.C. The spirits of presidents, First Ladies, and others are said to walk its halls—and sometimes interact with the current residents. Whether you believe in ghosts or not, it can be fun and interesting to learn about the stories. What do you think? Is the White House haunted?

SPOOKY STUFF

Slaves were among the workers who built the original White House. It wouldn't be surprising to find that their spirits linger there, too.

The White House is a very big building. It has 132 rooms, 147 windows, and 32 bathrooms.

-Mr. Burns's Ghost-

The original owner of the White House land might be its first ghost. A man named David Burns (sometimes reported as "Burnes") owned the land on which much of Washington, D.C., including the White House, would be built. He sold it to the government—but may never have really left! White House workers have reported hearing his voice saying "I'm Mr. Burns" from a few different rooms.

THE SCENT OF SOAP

Today, the East Room is a grand reception room used for press conferences, bill-signing ceremonies, and other events. Abigail Adams—the first First Lady to live in the White House—had another use for it: she used it to hang up the laundry! It was the warmest and driest room in the still-unfinished house.

In the many years since, a number of people have reported seeing the ever-practical Mrs. Adams still going about her laundry tasks in the White House, arms outstretched as if holding a basket. Some say the scents of clean laundry and soap (sometimes the flowery smell of lavender) accompany her. Even President Howard Taft himself said he thought he saw her ghost float through closed doors in the mansion.

ABIGAIL ADAMS

"Not a Single Apartment"

The new presidential mansion wasn't quite ready yet when its first occupants arrived. The second president of the United States, John Adams, moved in on November 1, 1800, and his wife, Abigail Adams, arrived a few days later. Mrs. Adams wasn't impressed. In fact, she wrote in a letter that, "There is not a single apartment finished. We have not the least fence, yard, or other convenience."

BURNING DOWN THE HOUSE

In 1812, the United States went to war with Great Britain again. By the latter half of 1814, many British forces were in America. On August 24, 1814, the British captured Washington, D.C., and burned many buildings—including the U.S. Capitol and the White House. President James Madison and his wife, Dolley Madison, fled just ahead of the soldiers.

When the Madisons returned, they lived in the nearby Octagon House, which has ghost stories of its own. The White House wasn't ready to be lived in again until 1817, by which time James Monroe was president. By that time, the presidential residence had gathered a new ghost: people told of the spirit of a British soldier who roams the grounds with a torch.

Some stories say the British soldiers, arriving at the White House, decided to sit down and eat a meal using the house's dishes. Only then did they set it on fire!

-OCTAGON HOUSE-

The Octagon House was the Washington home of a Virginia plantation owner named John Tayloe. While there are many ghost stories about the site, they may be later inventions. The ghosts of two of Tayloe's daughters **allegedly** linger there, and stories say they fell from the stairs after arguing with their father. However, there's little evidence this is true! Dolley Madison is also said to haunt the house.

DOLLEY AND THE ROSES

The living Dolley Madison may have had to flee the White House, but stories say her spirit may remain there still. However, the stories are a bit confused. While some say Dolley created the first White House Rose Garden, this is probably not actually the case. In truth, Mrs. Madison wasn't much of a gardener. The first Rose Garden was the work of Ellen Wilson, first wife of President Woodrow Wilson, in 1913.

However, that doesn't mean Dolley Madison didn't like roses. Perhaps that's why the legends say that her ghost appeared to protect the garden when First Lady Edith Wilson (President Wilson's second wife) planned to move it. The garden (which may have never been in danger at all) stayed where it was.

This photo shows the White House Rose Garden in 1921. There's no evidence that Edith Wilson ever really planned to move it.

SPOOKY STUFF

The confusion over the Rose Garden may have started because First Lady Edith Roosevelt (*not* Wilson) created a colonial garden at the White House in 1902. That was replaced with Ellen Wilson's garden in 1913.

THE SWEARING GHOST

President Andrew Jackson, known to be strong willed while he was alive, seems to continue to be so after death, at least according to many stories. Jackson, who served as president from 1829 to 1837, is one of the more commonly reported White House ghosts. During the 1860s, First Lady Mary Todd Lincoln said she'd heard Jackson stomping around and swearing in the White House. Many people have said they sense or hear him in the Rose Room.

President Harry Truman said he also envisioned Jackson as a ghost in the house. In fact, in a letter, he wrote: "The floors pop and the drapes move back and forth—I can just imagine old Andy (Jackson) and Teddy (Roosevelt) having an argument over Franklin (Roosevelt)."

When Jackson was **inaugurated** as president in 1829, many people followed him into the White House. The crowd trashed the place!

-What Truman Heard-

Truman, who was president from 1945 to 1953, said a number of times that he sensed ghosts in the White House. Once, he said, he heard knocking at his bedroom door, but there was no one there. He also heard footsteps. Interestingly, though, it was also during his presidency that people discovered the building needed a lot of repair work. That could provide some explanation of what he heard and sensed.

DEATHS IN THE WHITE HOUSE

In 1841, William Henry Harrison became the first U.S. president to die in office—and the first-known person to die in the White House. He'd only been president for 31 days when he died of what was believed to be **pneumonia**. His vice president, John Tyler, took over. However, Harrison's spirit is still said to haunt the White House's attic, reportedly looking for something.

The second White House death was only a little more than a year later. Letitia Tyler, wife of John Tyler, died of a stroke in September 1842. Tyler remarried Julia Gardiner in 1844, becoming the first president to marry while in office. John Tyler's ghost is now said to haunt the White House's Blue Room—in which he proposed to Julia.

This photo shows the Blue Room in the 1970s. It's used for receptions and was the site of the only wedding of a president and First Lady in the White House: Grover Cleveland and Frances Folsom in 1886.

SPOOKY STUFF

Ten people are known to have died in the White House, including William Henry Harrison and Letitia Tyler. Only one other president has died there: President Zachary Taylor in 1850.

A VERY SOLEMN SPIRIT

By far the most famous and well-known White House ghost stories have to do with the 16th president of the United States, Abraham Lincoln. Not only did Lincoln lead the country through the **upheaval** and heartbreak of the American Civil War, but his life and presidency ended very suddenly, taken by an **assassin** in April 1865 even as the war ended. Still, it was decades before anyone reported seeing or sensing Lincoln's ghost.

While President Calvin Coolidge was in the White House from 1923 to 1929, his wife, Grace Coolidge, said she saw Lincoln looking out a window in the Oval Office, out across the Potomac River. While she was the first person to say they saw or sensed Lincoln there, she certainly wasn't the last.

PRESIDENTS THEODORE ROOSEVELT, HERBERT HOOVER, AND DWIGHT EISENHOWER ALL REPORTED SEEING LINCOLN'S GHOST, AS DID FIRST LADIES JACQUELINE KENNEDY AND LADY BIRD JOHNSON.

IN THIS TEMPLE
AS IN THE HEARTS OF THE PEOPLE
FOR WHOM HE SAVED THE UNION
THE MEMORY OF ABRAHAM LINCOLN
IS ENSHRINED FOREVER

During President Franklin D. Roosevelt's long time in the White House, from 1933 to 1945, there were many reports of Lincoln's ghost. First Lady Eleanor Roosevelt said that she sensed him. Queen Wilhelmina of the Netherlands, staying in the Lincoln Bedroom in 1942, said that she answered a knock at the door and opened it to see Lincoln looking at her.

British Prime Minister Winston Churchill may have had the most amusing encounter. He said that he got out of his bath in the room only to find Lincoln standing by the fireside. Churchill, often hard to bother, reportedly said, "Good evening, Mr. President. You seem to have me at a disadvantage." Lincoln did not, apparently, respond. He just vanished. After that, Churchill apparently asked for a different room.

President Ronald Reagan's dog, Rex

In this photo, an actor portraying Abraham Lincoln sits in the White House in 2016, before a Halloween event.

Spooky Stuff

At least one White House employee said that President Ronald Reagan's dog wouldn't go into the Lincoln Bedroom. Instead, the animal would just stand outside and bark.

THE LOST CHILD

Sadly, the connection between the Lincoln family and ghosts in the White House may have begun with the death of one of Abraham and Mary Todd Lincoln's sons, Willie. The boy died of an illness called typhoid fever in 1862 in the White House. He was only 11 years old. Both his parents were heartbroken. Lincoln reportedly often visited the **crypt** where Willie was buried. There, he'd sit and cry.

Both President Lincoln and Mary Todd Lincoln reported seeing Willie in the days and years after his death. The First Lady said she saw him standing at the foot of her bed. People who worked for President Ulysses S. Grant, who served in the office from 1869 to 1877, also said they saw the boy.

Willie Lincoln died in the Prince of Wales Room. It's now the President's Dining Room.

This drawing shows the Lincoln family. Willie is in the middle.

Spooky Stuff

The Lincolns had four boys, but only one lived to be an adult. Their son Edward died when he was only four, and Thomas, or Tad, died at age 18.

CAT IN THE CAPITOL

The so-called **demon** cat of Washington, D.C., isn't just a ghost story of the White House. While it's supposedly been seen there, this **spectral** kitty (or maybe more than one) actually spends much of its time in the basement of the U.S. Capitol Building. The stories started back in the 1800s, probably in the time after the Civil War.

Night watchmen started telling tales of a black cat with glowing eyes that would start out normal size—and then grow to the size of a tiger before pouncing! There are some threads of truth in the tale. Workers did bring cats to the Capitol and White House to hunt mice and rats. It's easy to imagine that one continued doing its job long after death.

At some point over the years—probably around 1898, when the floor was replaced—a cat left a group of paw prints in the concrete of the small Senate **Rotunda**.

-A Bad Sign-

Some say the demon cat (often called "DC") often appears before tragic U.S. events, such as Lincoln's assassination, the 1929 stock market crash, the death of Franklin D. Roosevelt in 1945, and the assassination of President John F. Kennedy in 1963. Some also include appearances before the September 11, 2001, terrorist attacks and the landfall of **Hurricane** Katrina in 2005.

A DAUGHTER'S PLEA

While many people know that John Wilkes Booth assassinated President Lincoln, not as many people probably know that Booth and Lincoln weren't the only two who died as part of the scheme. Four other people were found guilty of **conspiracy** and hanged in 1865 for their alleged part in a plot to kill Lincoln and other leaders. One of those people was Mary Surratt.

MARY SURRATT

MARY SURRATT'S TRIAL TOOK PLACE IN THIS COURTROOM. SHE OWNED THE BOARDINGHOUSE WHERE THE CONSPIRATORS MET.

No one's really sure if Surratt was guilty, but her daughter, Anna, 22 at the time, was sure that Mary was innocent. Before the execution, she made her way to the White House, banging on the doors and begging President Andrew Johnson to spare her mother. It didn't work—and now, stories say, Anna's ghost arrives every year on the day her mother died, asking endlessly for mercy.

MAKING CONTACT

Many of the ghost stories of the White House date from around the time during and after the Civil War. There's a reason for that. People struggled to deal with the immense death toll and the fact that their loved ones often died far from home. Many turned to spiritualism, a belief that the spirits of the dead can speak to the living, and séances, meetings where the living try to contact the dead.

The residents of the White House weren't **immune** to the idea of spiritualism. Mary Todd Lincoln tried to contact the spirit of her son with a number of séances at the White House. These took place in the Red Room, one of the reception rooms in the White House.

SPOOKY STUFF

Many people died during the Civil War, which killed more Americans than any other war to date. About 750,000 people died in the war—maybe even more.

This photo shows the Red Room during the time of FDR. President Lincoln even attended a few séances in the Red Room—and after Lincoln's death, many people wanted to believe that his spirit lingered on, as well.

WASHINGTON HAUNTINGS

The White House and the U.S. Capitol aren't the only supposedly haunted places in Washington, D.C. There's a lot of history there, and where there's history, there are ghost stories! The former site of Mary Surratt's boardinghouse is said to be haunted, as is Lafayette Square, which was once home to slave markets and the site of a number of murders.

Saint John's Episcopal Church, near the White House, has a bell that stories say summons six spirits in white. The Old Post Chapel, near Arlington National **Cemetery**, has a ghostly lady in red. Decatur House supposedly has a ghost that cries out in pain after being injured in a duel. The Hay-Adams Hotel allegedly has a guest that never left after her death. There are so many stories it's impossible to list them all.

Stories say that when the huge church bell at Saint John's Episcopal Church rings after the death of a famous person, six figures appear in the president's pew at midnight. Then, they vanish.

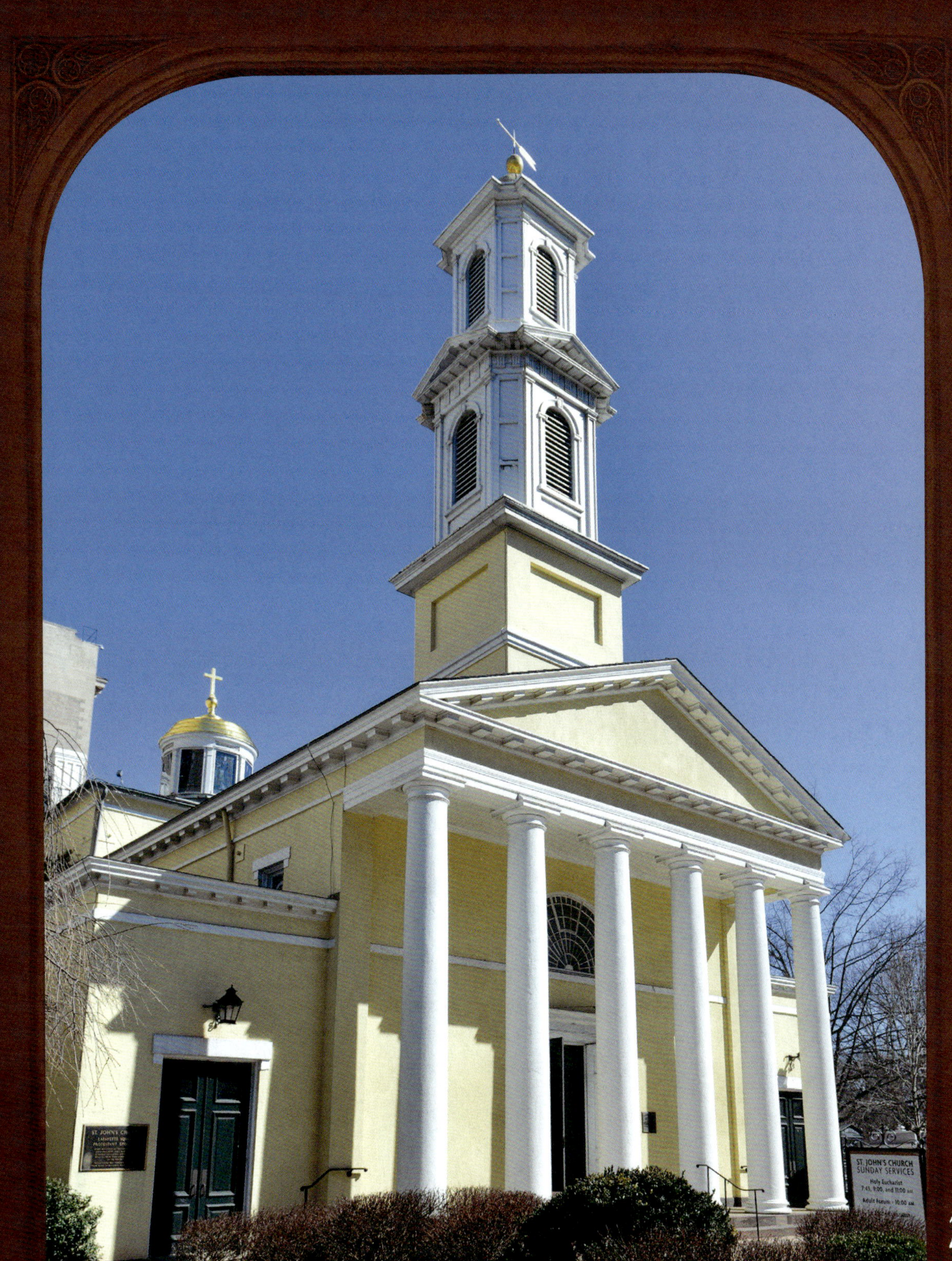
ST. JOHN'S CHURCH
SUNDAY SERVICES
Holy Eucharist

TIME MARCHES ON

For more than 220 years, the White House has been home to U.S. presidents and their families. Originally called the President's Palace and then the Executive Mansion, the big building on Pennsylvania Avenue has been rebuilt after wartime, seen life and death within its walls, been the site of decisions that have changed the United States and the world, and hosted all manner of events both light hearted and serious.

It's no surprise the White House has many ghost stories. It'd probably be more surprising if it didn't! It's kind of nice to imagine President Abraham Lincoln still looking after his country today, or to think of Dolley Madison strolling through the Rose Garden. After reading these stories, do you think the White House is haunted? Maybe it is!

GLOSSARY

allegedly: Said to have happened but not proven.

assassin: Someone or something that kills with a sudden attack.

cemetery: A place where the dead are buried.

conspiracy: The act of secretly planning to do something illegal or harmful.

crypt: A room, often under a church, where dead bodies are buried.

demon: An evil spirit.

hurricane: A powerful storm that forms over water and causes heavy rainfall and high winds.

immune: Not capable of being affected by something.

inaugurate: To introduce someone into a new position, such as that of president.

pneumonia: A serious sickness that affects the lungs.

rotunda: A large, round room, especially if covered with a dome.

spectral: Having to do with a ghost.

upheaval: A major change or time of change.

INDEX

WEBSITES

Due to the changing nature of Internet links, PowerKids Press has developed an online list of websites related to the subject of this book. This site is updated regularly. Please use this link to access the list: www.powerkidslinks.com/haunted/whitehouse